Sexy Short Stories to Read in Bed

Secret encounters

My Lip-biting Short Stories Series
- Book Two -

Alex Frack

WARNING

ACCESS TO THE SHORT STORIES CONTAINED IN THIS
VOLUME IS TO BE RESTRICTED TO AN ADULT AUDIENCE.

CONTENTS

ACKNOWLEDGMENTS

'Sexy Short Stories to Read in Bed' is a tested series of books for women, men and couples looking for classic easy-to-read erotica and sex stories with very explicit sex scenes.

Think about it. Don't we all need nice, steamy and sexy short stories that can be read in bed, right before sleeping to finish our day with a little bit of privacy and fun? Or even first thing in the morning to spice up your day, not to mention those long and boring commuting journeys where a little bit of sexy can... Well, you know.

'Sexy Short Stories to Read in Bed - Secret Encounters...' is the second volume in the series and proposes four short sex & erotica stories that will make you bite your lips. Perhaps even more...

The first short story *'And when you're done'* is the story

9

of a young married girl who needs a rough experience to spice up (and perhaps even save) her marriage. She goes online, finds an older man who seems in the same mood, and lets him take things to a level she did not imagine...

The second short story, *'Flashback'*, is about a flashback. A girl comes back home after years away and becomes the center piece of a welcome party. Until her eyes meet those of a man she had her first experience with years ago...

The third story, *'Massage'*, is about a steamy massage. A normal, innocent massage, that progressively becomes tempting and unbearable...

The fourth short story, *'James'* is the story of Nina, a single and lonely girl who decides to go on a sex experiment with a dominant man, next door. She lets him take control over her and... Well, you'll see!

Bonus story? Yes, there is a bonus sexy story in the end. steamy, explicit sex before going to bed...

As per the other book in this series, this short stories book is not about romance. The short stories build on love and cheeky needs but go straight to the point and contain very explicit sex scenes. They are written to be read easily and rapidly, in five to ten minutes, again and again.

If you are looking for a little bit of selfish sexy fun every once in a while, my book was made for you!

Oh, but of course reading them out-loud is also an option if you are not alone ... Your choice!

Cheekily yours...

Alex.

1 | AND WHEN YOU'RE DONE...

Don't get me wrong, I love my husband. I really do. But when it comes to sex, things have not been working well enough. I mean, we have sex. Great sex, loving sex. But he and I have very opposite views on the notion of fantasies.

Mine is 'treat me like a queen, fuck me like a whore'. Jonathan treats me like a queen, loves me like a queen, even eats me like a queen, but he refuses to do more. He sees me as a mother, respects women too much to dare... fucking me nasty. He won't go rough, never. He won't pull my hair, won't push me, won't make me yell, won't play beyond cuddles and loving sex.

So I've decided to, well, get some attention anyway.

I downloaded an app for people looking for dates and left a message there. Different guys replied. Some offered to get brutal. *Really? What's wrong with you people?* Some went on talking and talking. *Nope, thank you...* Others wanted a simple night out. *Still nope, sorry...* Until that guy showed up, looking for the same thing as I did. Well, sort of, obviously. The other way around. His wife would not let him play and he needed... that. He was a bit older, ten years more than me. But banging a younger girl made part of his fantasy. *Why not.*

So we talked. Not too much, just enough to decide. We exchanged a couple of emails, decided to get on a cam, to... well, check each other out. I insisted on doing that in the dark, terrified of being recognized or even recorded, but he undressed, asked to see more skin. And of course, things went a little bit out of control. He got hard staring at my bra, and I got excited looking at his... manhood. And so we both ended up caressing and having fun on our side of the screen. I loved watching him cum, loved knowing I was the cause of that. But after the action, we felt so awkward that we switched off and stopped talking to each other for a while. Silence.

Last week came with a surprise. An email, actually, asking me if I was still interested in doing this. I replied.

We considered our options. I wanted some place

neutral yet we didn't want to get this done in a cheap hotel. We talked about taboos and limits too. None for me, I wanted it hard and rough. So did he. Blowjobs? *Hell yes, dirty ones even.* Anal? *Hmmm, that would be a first, we'll see.*

Anyway, we planned a drink and booked a table in a fancy hotel the day after. Which basically is today. Sunday.

I didn't sleep much, felt guilty yet very excited. I went to see my friend Emy to get my legs waxed. And my bikini too, actually. Then I spent an hour choosing my outfit, tried five dresses and ten underwear sets before opting for a white ample skirt and a light shirt. I came back home twice, once after realizing that I forgot to take a condom and another after thinking that maybe one wouldn't be enough.

Then I took a taxi and headed for that bar.

I met him in the street. He kindly helped me get out of the cab. He seemed delicate. Definitely ten years older than me but elegant, with peppery hair. *Hmmm, not bad actually...* He took my arm and brought me inside.

He got me a large seat in the lobby's bar and looked at me as I crossed my legs. Then his eyes dropped

into my top, looking for my bra. *Weird at first but...*
Right, let's open one more button, you're here to fuck me, boy.
My move made him smile. His smile made me bite
my lip and giggle. *He's totally gonna fuck me.*

He talked to me for about ten minutes. His eyes
stayed locked on mine. You wouldn't normally sustain
that kind of look. Four seconds maybe, five tops. But
I played. His eyes explored mine, he eventually started
babbling, more focused on my eyes than on his actual
conversation. And I wasn't listening anyway.

Then he stood up, came close to me, still looking into
my eyes. He checked my legs and boobs on the way,
of course, but he made eye contact again. He was so
close. I bet I would have heard him whispering
despite the noise. He probably would have heard my
heart beat, actually. And our eyes made it all. Not
even a word.

"I need to have you now."

"I know."

"Wow, your boobs..."

"I know."

"And those legs..."

His hand got on my knee, caressed it gently.

"I know."

"So what do we do now?"

Still, silence, not a single word, his eyes were burning, the room temperature was becoming unbearable. I opened my collar a little more, tried to find some air around. *None, pfieww.* Then our silent eye-to-eye discussion started again.

"So what do we do now, beautiful girl?"

"I don't see too many options here, you're gonna have to do what has to be done..."

"Fuck you?"

I broke the silent discussion with a simple nod. He took my hand, I followed. He went into a corridor, opened a couple of doors. People saluted him. *Wait, what?*

"Hello Mr Director." - *Whaaaat? He's the boss?!*

Then he took my waist gently and guided me into a locked area of the hotel. Paint boxes, scaffolding everywhere. But no workers. *Of course, Sunday means no workers. Hmmm, clever boy...* He locked several doors after us, the whole thing was becoming the hottest afternoon ever. And then, a suite. Perfect, huge, a leaving room, two bedrooms, even an office.

I looked around, enjoying the feeling of his eyes on me. The guy probably knew my curves, legs and butt by heart now. And I still didn't know his name.

And then he pinned me against the wall. *Thank god, at last...* He crossed my hands on top of my head with one hand, pulled my waist to him with the other, grabbed my butt on the way. And then he broke the silence rule.

"Now I'm gonna fuck you, beautiful young lady."

I looked into his eyes and nodded in silence, merely whispered a 'ssshhhh'.

Then I talked to his ear, my body pressed against his.

"No talking, just fuck me the hardest you can, and when you're done just keep fucking me harder... love me like a queen, fuck me like a whore..."

He smiled and tightened his grip on my hands, his eyes burning with lust. He made me take my shoes off and unzipped my skirt behind my back before letting it fall on the floor. His eyes deep inside mine, his plunged his free hand inside my panties, went straight inside me. I groaned, screamed as his finger invaded me, stuck my head inside his shoulder.

"You're wet."

"Shhh" - *I know, fuck me.*

"Very wet" - *Will you fuck the hell out of me?!*

A second finger slipped inside me, making me groan inside his shoulder as he released my hands and grabbed my neck. I wrapped my arms around his shoulders, scratched his neck with my nails. A third finger joined in, making me scream, but his hand in my neck kept me firmly against him, restricting my body's urge to arch back.

He lifted me, carried me onto the desk, ordered me to raise my arms and took my top off on the way. I maintained eye contact, saw him look at my chest with even more lust in his eyes than before. His hands went straight inside my bra, grabbing squeezing and kneading my breasts as if they belonged to him.

"Tie your hair."

I took my bra off, massaged my boobs in silence before moaning. And I tied my hair. His eyes looked into mine. *I know, I'm a good girl, now fuck me!* Then he looked at my breasts as they moved up, and opened his pants.

I bit my lip again, looked at his boxer, squeaked in surprise looking at the huge hard shape inside it. *Oh my, this is going inside me?* Then he pushed me down on my knees. I grabbed the shape in his boxers with both hands, tried to feel it, then pulled the boxers down his legs, grabbing his butt and kissing his stomach with a moan. The boxer released his cock, gigantic, covered in little veins, clean-shaven, nearly hard as a rock. *I bet that's why you don't nail her too hard, my god, poor girl!*

I moved my head to the side and looked up into his eyes as I took his shaft with both hands. I began moving my hands on him, played with his balls on the way, sucking them, swallowing them. My hands rubbed the head of his cock, making it big and beautiful as my tongue moved from his base up to the tip, following a vein. Our eyes were still locked, I teased, played, forced him to react. My tongue ran behind the head, licked his tip, even cleaned a drop. *Fuck me.*

Then he grabbed my head and forced his cock inside my mouth. *Hmmm, at laaaast.* His cock felt huge on my tongue, huge inside my hands. I looked up and nodded. *Do it.* And he took control, pushed his cock deeper into my mouth, holding my head and neck. His cock then got inside my throat, harder, deeper. I gagged, but he kept pushing. I held on his butt, crushing it in my hands but fully letting him play. *Fuck me, and when you're done, fuck me again.* And then he groaned. He fucked my throat once more, his body crispated, he groaned, and he exploded inside my mouth, holding my head to stay as deep as possible. My hands crushed his body, I screamed feeling his cum flooding my tongue, then I came too, soaking my panties like never before.

He released me, looked into my eyes. I twirled my tongue around his cock, waiting for more eye contact quiet communication. He played my silence game, his eyes into mine.

"Thanks so much."

I took his cock in my hands again, sucked it more, cleaned it carefully. Then I smiled and swallowed his orgasm with a wink.

"You're welcome, boy."

"You're a bitch, aren't you."

I released his cock with a sonorous kiss.

"I know."

Then, still in the outmost silence, I turned around. I offered my hips, my butt, and looked at him over my shoulder. His cock was still hard, I shook my butt and looked at him, letting my eyes do the job.

"Now fuck me more."

"Bitch..."

He got on his knees and took place behind me. I looked at him over my shoulder, wiggled my butt.

"Come on boy! Fuck that pussy!"

He answered by taking my waist and spreading my knees. His cock slipped inside me. *Fuck he's so, so, so big.* He pushed, pushed more. My pussy was soaked but way too tight for his monster. He pushed, I screamed, tried to move away. *N..ooo, let me go, you're too...* But he kept me there, pulled my hair, got deeper inside me. *Fuuuuuuckkkk.* My pussy torn apart, stars in my eyes, my voice broke as his cock brutalized me. Then he slapped my butt harshly, pushed, even more, deeper, harder. My hands grabbed the carpet, I started yelling.

Then I came. Collapsed on the floor, tears in my eyes. I tried to catch my breath, giggled as if drunk. And I heard his voice, somehow, somewhere.

"We're not done, young lady"

I turned my head.

"What?"

"You said, when you're done, fuck me again and again"

His huge cock moved out of my pussy, rubbed my ass for a second. It made me scream. *Oh my god I'm so empty now.* Then he came inside me again, made me scream more. *Fuck, fuck, fuck!* And his finger began playing with my butt. *Oh my god, he's gonna kill me.*

"No, wait, wait!"

He grabbed my neck, pushed my face down, slipped a finger inside my ass.

"Love me like a queen, fuck me like a whore, right?"

"Hhhhhhhhhhhh"

"Then let's fuck you like a whore, my queen"

And then his fingers invaded my butt, took that remaining part of virginity nobody touched before. He fingered it gently but deeply, then harder. I screamed in pain and screamed again, but then I groaned. *Fuck this is sooo gooood!* And my hand grabbed his. And I began to scream at him.

"Fuck it!"

"Sorry?"

"Fuck it!!!"

"Beg your pardon?" - *Right, he's playing.*

"Fuck my fucking butt!!!"

And the end began. His cock slipped out from my pussy, made me groan again, and pushed to invade me differently. He held my chest and my waist harder than never and slipped fully inside me, making me tremble and yell louder than never in my life. He moved inside me, stretched me, made my body and legs electric. My nails scratched the wooden floor, I screamed as his cock took possession of me again, again, and again. My body shook, collapsed. More tears came out of my eyes as my brain literally exploded. I felt like a fuck doll, trapped in his arms, filled like never and fucked without limits like a queen whore. My legs collapsed too, making him deeper inside me. The orgasm made me shake, took my brain and speech away as he flooded me brutally with cum for a second time today.

I remained on the floor for a while, my brain out, completely incapable of talking, thinking, reacting to anything. He then pulled me on top of him, kissed my forehead and wrapped his arms around me. Our bodies were pressed one against another, our legs caressing each other. Our eyes met again, and our silent communication game took over.

"Fuck me, brutalise me, make me scream like a whore, make me cum, make me cry, but then love me and protect me like the

Queen I am?"

He looked deep into my eyes, like no other before, scrutinized them, explored my soul in silence. Then his hand caressed my cheek and pushed my hair away. He kissed my lips and, locking his eyes into mine, he nodded.

2 | FLASHBACK

Tonight is a very special night. I recently came back to my hometown after ten years abroad. I left soon after my 20th birthday because I wanted to see the world, and that was the best decision I ever took. I've seen things I never thought I'd see, met people I never thought I'd meet, and loved people I never thought I'd love. But I'm back home now, ready to start a new life, excited to see my friends again.

And I'm late! It is 9pm, and my cab has been stuck in traffic for way too long.

The evening takes place at my parents' place. They invited my closest friends, including my besties Anna and Josephine, who hates her name and makes faces when not called Jo. It's supposed to be a close circle night but I've done my best to look great, put on a dress and some elegant heels. I want them to see how much I've changed in ten years. No more baggy trousers, sweaters and sports shoes... But still, I'm terrified. *Hope they'll like the new me...*

Third floor. I ring the doorbell. I can feel and hear some agitation behind that door. *This is strange...* My father opens the door, gives me the most beautiful smile ever and takes me in his arms, squeezes my so hard I can't even breathe! *Yes Dad, I'm back and I love you too! Now please let me breathe!!!* My Mom joins, takes us in her arms too, tears in her eyes. *Awww, but Mom! Don't...!'*

OK, now I'm crying. And then I notice that the whole living room is full of people! The girls are here, and the neighbors, and my cousins, and... They all smile at me and welcome me with the greatest kindness ever. *Oh my, how did I actually live so far for so long?* My Dad disappears, opens some bottles as the girls scream and run into my arms. And then he comes back with a glass of champagne and gently makes me sit in his favorite armchair.

The evening goes on, friends smile, laugh with me, embrace me. And then my heart freezes. Jacob is right there, sitting in front of me, looking at me in silence, waving with a smile. *Oh, my, god! Jacob!*

Jacob and I have known each other for a long time.

He's my father's best friend, has been there for me since I was a child and has always looked after me. He picked me up at the police station a couple of times without telling my father, after a got into a fight or two. *Yeah, that used to be me.* He was also here when boys dumped me and I needed a shoulder to cry on. In short, he's always made sure I would be ok, or better than ok.

But then we slept together. Once. The night right before I left the country.

I'd spent that last evening at my parents' place. My Dad had planned everything from the dinner pizza to the time departure for the airport in the morning. Jacob had spent the afternoon with my parents, and was actually devastated as his wife had just filed for divorce. She'd met someone apparently, and had left him without much of an explanation.

When I came home after an afternoon with the girls, Dad and Jacob were having a drink. I went for a shower and heard the door slam after Dad had shouted that he had to go pick up Mom. But when I went out of the bathroom, Jacob was there, sitting on the couch, a drink in his hand.

I'm not sure why, but things turned hot very fast.

I wrapped a towel around my chest and went to talk to him. I took the glass from his hands, and put it away from him on the table.

"Jacob, stop drinking, you've had enough."

Of course, he didn't agree, so I slipped my fingers inside his fingers and straddled him, on the couch. He looked at me with so much surprise in his eyes.

"Honey, what are you..."

"Jacob, shhhhhh…"

I put a finger on his lips, then slipped my hands into his hair and guided him into my neck. He fought me for a little while but then gave up as I wrapped my arms around his neck, my body against his. He then started kissing my shoulders, grabbed my hips, caressed my hair. He looked into my eyes, and I kissed him too.

We barely talked. I opened my towel, still straddling him, made him look at me. I dropped the towel, took his hands and placed them on my chest, moaned as he caressed my breasts in silence. I straightened my back and got my boobs in front of his mouth, gave him the choice to play or not. He did, started to lick my tits, nibbled at them. I guided his hand inside my legs, made him play with his fingers, moaned as he spread my pussy lips, moaned as he slipped his fingers inside me. I let his hands run on me, my chest, my back and butt. I kept his face against me, groaned as his mouth played more with my tits. Then I unbuckled his pants and grabbed his cock inside.

I walked away for a minute, locked the door so no one could come in the flat, and came back. I pulled his pants, kneeled, and took him in my mouth, played with his cock, blew air on it, then blew it, felt him with my tongue, on my tongue, inside my cheeks. And deeper, inside my throat, eyes in the eyes.

First blow job ever. Big time.

He played with my hair, looked at me.

"Calm down honey, no rush, just... take your time... "

I could feel my heart pound in my chest so hard, but I calmed down, sucked him slow and soft. Probably clumsy. But he became very hard, moaned, guided my head with one finger, helped me with the pace. His cock was delicious, throbbing, sensitive, reactive. Extremely reactive. I took him deeper again, played with my tongue, moaned as my fingers began to play between my legs.

Then the elevator rang, my parents were there, right outside the door. My Mom was laughing, seemingly teasing my Dad.

Jacob panicked, tried to move. But it moved his cock even deeper in my mouth and made me gag. Then I jumped on him, straddled him again, my hand keeping his mouth shut.

The key turned inside the door lock as I lowered my hips and made the tip of his cock slip on my clit, slide inside me. I squeaked, kept my hand on his mouth, and got him deeper inside me.

"Pizzas guys!"

But the security locker prevented the door from opening. I moved on him, felt him inside me, deep inside me. His hands crushed my boobs, grabbed my butt and my hips. Our mouths met, our tongues mixed. And as the door banged in the security lock for the fifth or sixth time Jacob filled me with an orgasm, precisely as my pussy exploded.

The door covered my scream, then my Dad started ringing the bell and called us for help. I moved away from Jacob, grabbed my towel and went straight to the bathroom as he'd put his pants back on and rushed to the door, pretending he'd fallen asleep after too many drinks.

"Sweetheart, are you ok?"

I am back at the party. Probably after a little absence. My Dad is gently caressing my cheek, pouring more champagne in my glass.

"Hi Dad, sure, I'm great!"

I stand, take him into my arms and kiss his cheek as he takes me in his arms. Over his shoulder, my eyes meet Jacob's. I feel his eyes on me, ten years later. He looks at my dress and heels, discretely checks my legs, and smiles at me as I bit my lips.

Then my Dad released me, turned around, filled Jacob's glass and took him away laughing. I'm sure of two things, though. Jacob just had the same flashback, and my girly panties were so wet I had no choice but to sit back and cross my legs...

3 | MASSAGE

I am tired. My day has been long, and because I do massages as a job I stand almost all the time. My back hurts, my neck is stiff, but I still need to take care of my last client. Then I can take off for a drink with the girls.

I love my job though. I release people from stress, most of the clients are nice and I never have to deal with grumpy customers. I even get to lay my eyes on beautiful and muscular bodies... And when that happens I usually can't resist getting an eyeful. But hey, not more! Gosh, I've considered grabbing a butt here and then but... *Hmmm. No, that would be so unprofessional.*

I open the spa door. The lights are soft, there is a relaxing music playing at the back and a little fountain. Very Feng Shui, the clients love that room. I wash my hands and move towards the client, who is nearly falling asleep on the work table. His shoulders are large, is back is strong, his legs shaven. *Must be a swimmer.* And his lower back is covered with a white towel, like always.

I bend towards his ear and lay my hand on his back softly.

"Good evening Sir, I am Kate and I will begin your massage. Please just relax, no need to talk."

I turn around and pour some oil in my hands, then move around him. I begin with his back, run my thumbs softly down his spine. He moans softly, then I open my palms and cover his back with the oil. My fingers insist on tensed muscles for a couple of minutes, then move on his legs. He jumps. *Oops, sorry, that must be sensitive.* I press my hands on his calves, try to relax his muscles. *Shhhh, just relax.* Then I move up on his tights, release the pressure, move down slowly to his feet. I pour more oil into my hands and massage them. He reacts again. I gently apply pressure on his calves, work on his feet. *Damn you are so tense, relax boy.*

He moans softly but eventually lets me do. Then I turn around him and massage his arms, his large shoulders, his strong arms, down to his hands. The palm, then the fingers.

At this stage, most clients fall asleep. That's the part of my work I prefer. But he doesn't. I rub his neck softly, he groans, then moves again onto his back.

I feel tensions disappear, he moans. Then his hand weakly grabs my side.

"Down, please, down..."

My hands are on the edge of the towel.

"Sir, I'm sorry, I..."

"Down, please..."

I bite my lip. *Damn, why are you doing this to me?*

Then he moves his arm, pushes the towel down, gives me access to his butt. *Oh, my, he's not wearing the paper underwear. Boy, this butt is the cutest...* I massage his lower back, press my fingers, flirt a little bit with his skin. Then I begin massaging his butt, with my oily palms, from his lower back to his tights. My heart beats accelerate, my fingers feel him, I bite my lips and squirm. He moans, relaxed. I feel wet, so wet.

A couple of squeaks later, after minutes of massaging that beautiful ass, I put the towel back into place. Then I bend to the client's ear. *Now you calm down boy, that's enough.*

"Please turn around when you are ready, Sir."

He moans, makes a noise, struggles to turn around, keeps his eyes closed. I hold the towel into place as he moves, then oil my hands again.

I start with his feet again, then move up his legs, pressing my thumbs in the middle of his calves all the way up. I turn around him, focus on his strong shoulders and arms. Then I add more oil and massage his torso. Clean-shaven, muscular. And a six-pack. My hands run on his sides, keep relaxing him for a minute or two.

Then I bite my lips and flirt with his lower stomach. Most clients don't like being touched there and we never go there anyway. But, well, he'd turned me on and my panties were all wet. I need to try.

So I run my fingers under the towel, feel his shaven skin centimeter by centimeter. Until my fingers reach his base. Then I flirt a little more.

"Hmm, what?"

"Nothing Sir, just relax, all is good..."

I fight with myself, bite my lips and resist from getting my hand right inside my panties. I push the towel away instead. He doesn't react.

More oil on my hands. His cock is big, long, beautiful. My hand take his shaft and put it on his stomach, flat, before massaging him. My greasy fingers run on each side of the cock, teasing it, firmly but softly, making him bigger and harder, my other hand cupping his balls.

His cock becomes hard, straightens up. I release the head, blow air on it, then circle my fingers around it and pull them down to his base. Left hand, right hand. His cock begins throbbing, his eyes remain close. *No, bad idea, don't do it. Don't do that! Oh, fuck it. Do it.*

I bend, take his head in my mouth. Just a taste. I twirl my tongue around the head, swallows him, allows my lips to reach his Base. *Oh my god, I carve this cock.*

He moans, groans. Tries to hold my head on his cock. My hand softly pushes his hands away, I let his cock go. I moan, squirm. *He's delicious, fuck!* Then I move my hands faster on him, up and down, down and up. He groans, grabs the table, opens his eyes, looks at me, is eyes asking for an orgasm. He blushes, goes red. And so do I.

"Shhh, just relax, Sir."

His hand grabs my butt, crushes it.

I play, slow down the pace. My left hand holds his firmly while my free hand teases the tip, makes him harder and harder.

Damn, he's cumming so hard! I keep rubbing his cock, twirl my fingers around the head, block his scream with my hand, keep him as silent as possible while a wave of cum erupts, covering my hand. Then a second, a third, and a fourth. I keep playing, keep him company as he shakes on my table, let him cover my hands with his abundant white liquid.

Then he collapses, releases my butt and remains silent. I close my eyes, catch my breath, put the towel back on him, pick some tissues and leave the room in silence, my heart pounding in my chest.

When I left work twenty minutes later my panties were soaked and my mind obsessed with his fabulously throbbing cock. I met my manager in the corridor.

"Hi Kate! How did it go with Mr Peters?" *Shit, she knows, I'm so fired!*

"Hi, it went well, I think... Why ? Did he complain?". *Oh my, please tell me that son of a bitch didn't complain.*

"No! He loved you and said he'd come back for the same. Guess you just got yourself a regular client!"

Stay calm. Don't show.

"Oh, well, I'm glad then" *Hmmm. Me, I guess.*

"Great, good night then! Still going out with the girls tonight?"

"Sure!" *But definitely not now. My pussy needs way too much care right now, the girls will have to wait...*

4 | JAMES

Today is my day off. The first one in a long while. I was supposed to spend it with my best friend Amelia, but she cancelled ten minutes ago with a text: "Fabio arrived without warning, day in bed, sorry!". In other words, my friend is having some fun instead of spending her day with me. *And I'm fucking alone!*

So I'm chilling, my steaming coffee in one hand, a towel wrapped around my waist after a quick shower which, if I'd known, could have turned into a long bubble bath. *Damn it.*

My own man is gone, I have been single for six months now and I have no one to look after me. Yet, I look in the mirror and what I see is not unpleasant. My long hair hides a firm and round chest, my stomach is flat, my butt is... yes, firm too. Well, my bikini line is not as smooth as when a boy used to spend time down there, but hey... it's sweet under the fingers, and... it's life. Speaking of fingers... *hmm*... I miss that feeling too. *Hey, what if I got myself some naughty sex, after all?*

A clip in my hair, some panties caught on the way, I sit on my bed and switch my laptop on.

A website caught my eye some time ago, something to make your fantasies real... *Oh, there it is. Let's see...*

So! I'm... *a woman*... looking for... *a man*. For real or fantasy online? *For real.*

A list of fantasies shows up. A cop, a teacher, in a public place... *not convinced, let's try something else.* A stranger? *Good start.* Rather sweet or cheeky? *Definitely cheeky.* Dominant? *Never tried this, hmmm, why not...*

A profile pops up. His name is James, 35 years old. Single. He seems a nice guy. I click, look through his profile. A small window opens.

"Hello, I'm James."

"Nina."

"Interested in meeting someone, Nina?" - *Damn, he's on a rush or what? Ok, let's have some fun.*

"Why not…"

"Single?"

"Yep."

"Horny?" - *Hey! What the... Who do you think you are?!*

Silence.

"Used to get naughty sex with strangers?" - *Obviously not, otherwise I wouldn't need this site. What does he think? Ok, don't be stupid, play along...*

"Yes, I'm a big girl..." - *Well, a tiny lie won't harm.*

"Brunette? Blonde? Redhead?"

"Brunette."

"Small? Tall? Slim? Curvy?"

"Slim, tall, nice shapes..."

"Tiny breasts?" - *Gosh, is he a cop or what?*

"Medium, nice boobs..." - *Are you finished now?*

"Shaved apricot?" - *Ouch, if you knew dear... I don't have a boyfriend and it's quite wild down there! Hasn't been an apricot for a while... Ok, let's see how he reacts.*

"Unfortunately for you, no ..."

Silence. *He doesn't seem inspired... Oh, no, there he is!*

"Have you ever let a stranger play with your body? As he wishes, I mean. "

"No..."

I bite my lips, I want more. And my left-hand slips gently inside my thighs to reach my panties.

"Shy girl then? I thought I was talking to a big girl who dares..."

"Aie. Yes, right. Let's say, a big girl who... "

"Curious?"

"Yes, curious."

"Horny curious?"

"Horny curious."

"Dressed-up?"

"Hey! Wait, you're the only one asking here, it's not fair!"

"Dressed-up? Answer!"

"In my panties, sitting on my bed."

Silence.

"You see the plan at the top of your screen?"

"Yes why?"

"We're almost neighbors, we could..." - *Ouch! I just bit my lip, what an idiot!*

"When?"

"Now... in 15 minutes..." - *Wow, but I'm not gonna go on a date with a jungle down there...*

"Gosh ... no ... I must, you know."

"Shave? Don't worry, I don't care... Do you have black stockings though?" - *Oh my, is he serious?*

" Yes, of course, why? Does it compensate for the bush?"

"Let's say 20 minutes... the white building facing the bridge..."

The connection is off, he's gone. I wonder. I'm excited, my panties leave no doubt about that. I slip a finger, I'm soaked, my lips swollen with excitement. I bite my lip, moans and collapse on my bed. My fingers push my white cotton panties, tease, spread, enter. I melt, moan, grab a pillow, squeak, cum in minutes. *Hmm, promising...*

Oh my! I'm late! I get up, replace my cotton panties with a dry black thong, put on my stockings, a skirt, a matching bra, a tank top and a clip in my hair. *Don't forget your teeth, very important.* My purse... my keys ... *Go on Nina!*

I'm at the bridge. The white building is impossible to miss, but the street is empty. I look around, nobody. I lean on the wall, looking for my phone.

"Wow!"

Someone is taking my waist behind me, I jump and scream.

"Nina? James."

I turn around, look at him in the eyes. He offers a hand, looks at me with his green eyes, then kisses my cheek. The corner of the lips actually. His accent is light, rather charming. Short beard, redhead, clear eyes.

"I'm glad to meet you, Nina."

I smile, look for my words, baffle. He doesn't seem to care, pulls me closer and takes me into the building. Then he pins me on the wall, wraps his hands around me, feels my curves , grabs my butt, my boobs.

"So you can either come up and spend the day with me or go away free..."

I smile, caress his cheek for an answer. Our tongues mix, he pulls my top up, his hands move on my back. He looks into my eyes, seems to expect me to say something. We're in the building's hall, I need to get somewhere private.

"So can you take the lead, James?"

He bites my lip, detaches himself from me and opens another door. Second floor, no lift, the gentleman lets me go first. To enjoy the view without a doubt. He grabs my butt again. I slap his hand.

"Shhh, James! Wait!"

Second floor. James opens a door.

"Please Nina, come in." - *No, I'm freaking out. But I am horny and this situation turns me on so much.*

"Sure, thanks."

He opens the door, lets me into a beautiful and bright apartment decorated with taste. A bachelor's place, books, a vintage playboy magazine cleverly displayed on a coffee table. I go in, take a few steps, look around. He takes my wrist softly, stops me right there.

"Take off your shoes, please."

Okay... I obey, leave my purse on the floor. He looks

at me with a smile as I remove my ballerinas. I feel his eyes on me, my legs, my butt. *He's getting addicted.*

Then I continue my visit. I enter the living room, let my eyes run over the books, open the playboy magazine with a smile as I notice girls from the 90's with big breasts and big bushes. *Now, I get him.* Then I jump again, feeling his hands on my hips.

"Take this off, Nina."

He pulls on my skirt.

"And that."

Then on my top.

"And do not argue."

I turn, look into his eyes, then silently unbutton my skirt and pull off my top. His eyes rest on my chest, he examines my bra, caresses the top of my breasts.

"Turn around".

I obey, look at him in silence while his eyes examine me. He caresses my hips, my butt, my stockings, then disappears. I continue my visit in silence, both excited and anxious.

I find a mirror, see a pretty brunette in black lingerie

in there. I look at myself, happy with my look, then jump for the third time as his hands grab my shoulders.

"James! Stop scaring me!"

"From now on, you are mine. Do not say anything, just let me do. If you talk, I stop and it's over. Do we have a deal, Nina?"

I nod silently, looking him in the eyes.

"Sit down on this table."

I obey. James lays a small silk handkerchief under my butt. I cross my legs and watch him open a small leather case, from which he takes a small chisel and a razor.

"Spread your legs Nina."

Seriously? So the plan was to make my bush clean? I obey, shudder. He caresses my stockings, my thighs, then examines my thong closely. His fingers slide along the thong, then he removes it. Without even worrying about my reaction, he passes his hand on my bikini hair, then makes me spread my legs wide. *Oh, my, this is weird. Exciting weird.*

I swallow, bite my lip at the idea of being wide open on a perfect stranger's dining table. His fingers run on my skin, his chisel starts cutting, shortening. Then he pours oil on his hands and undertakes to spread it on my pussy. His fingers brush against my lips, I close my eyes, moan. His hands close on my ankles, firmly.

"Shhh Nina, in silence."

He straightens up, grabs his razor, then meticulously begins to free my skin. In a few passages, my bikini area is perfectly silky. His hands keep moving, he spreads my tights and looks at his work, while cleaning the blade. His fingers drive me crazy, brush my clit, his face only a couple of inches from me.

James places a small mirror between my legs, shows me a perfectly clean pussy.

"Everything fine?"

I look at him, check the result with my fingers, still wide open on the table, his eyes staring at my open and bald pussy. I bite my lips, nod, he takes a step back and looks at me.

"Get your top off now."

I blush but I obey. I cross my legs, try to hide my chest.

"I want you naked and wide open on my table Nina."

I look at him, then silently move back on the table. But my legs remain crossed. *Happy to obey but not too much.* He comes closer, runs his fingers over my body, teases the tip of my breasts. I moan, bite my lip, wiggle my butt. He puts my hands behind me, opens my legs.

"From now, you stop moving."

His fingers slide on my stomach, then he caresses my hips, my butt. He lifts me up, pulls me towards him and separates my knees.

"Close your eyes."

I obey. His fingers take possession, rub my clit, slip inside me. I can't stay in place, I squirm, try not to moan. He caresses my thighs, then his mouth closes on my clit. *Hmm, James!* His tongue slips between my tiny lips, he sucks me, nibbles. *Shhh, don't speak, say nothing!*

I run my hands through his hair, moan louder. I try to catch my breath and grab his wrist, look him in the eyes, bite my bottom lip. *James, slow down, I'm coming too fast, too loud, I beg you, slow down.* But he smiles. His fingers turn around and curl up inside me. I scream, my body arches, I turn around on the table, hold on to the edges. *Fuuuuck!*

He grabs my throat, stares at me, then slips a third finger inside me. He invades, pounds. I'm on fire, ready to explode. I tremble, I shake, I scream. His fingers force me to orgasm, thirty minutes after meeting me, undressing me and shaving me clean.

Time to catch my breath. James stands and sits on a wide sofa. He leaves me wide open and shaking on his table, looks at me, then asks me to come to him. I obey, he makes me kneel before him, on a comfortable cushion, then he unfastens his belt.

"Your turn now."

I look at him, to force him to speak his mind.

"Undress me, and suck me."

He leans over, kisses me, runs his fingers through my hair, grabs my breasts roughly, then pushes my face towards his cock. The thing is already half out of his boxer, he guides me to it and slips it between my lips before lowering his hand right between my thighs. I hold on to his sides, he swells on my tongue, but his fingers invade my clit again. I pull out in a moan, stick my forehead inside his shoulder. I bite his arm, push him back, straighten up, chest bulging, too proud to obey without showing that I remain master of my actions. I pass my hand on his boxer and takes his cock. He lifts his waist, helps me to pull the pants down.

"Suck me, Nina."

I stare at him, continue my game, decide to disobey.

"Close your eyes, James."

"You're cheating."

I raise my hands.

"Close your eyes, otherwise you get nothing, obey."

James looks at me with a smile, then closes his eyes. I lower his boxer, release him, take it with both hands. I lean over, gently gobble his balls, then allow my tongue up along his hard shaft. I straighten my back, move my mouth away from him. He opens his eyes, grumpy.

"Close your eyes or I go."

"Suck me, I give the orders."

I gently pat his cock as an answer. It pops like a spring, then I push on his tights and pretend to get up.

"Ok, you win."

James decides to obey me, I giggle and wiggle, take his cock back inside my mouth. My left hand slips between my thighs, the right one comes and goes on him. My tongue tickles him, then I swallow him all at once. I push James a little deeper into my mouth, then into my throat. I begin a sweet and deep back and forth movement. My lips slip from the tip of his head down to his base. he is entirely inside me, stretches, swells, widens, hardens.

I look at him, our eyes meet. I resume, enjoy this indecent game. My fingers close on my clit, I wiggle and groan, excited with the idea of making a stranger totally crazy in my mouth. *Nina, Nina, what are you doing?* Then his hands slip into my hair.

"After that, I'm going to fuck you, and you'll be an obedient brunette again."

"Shut up, James."

James straightens up, takes my head in his hands and leads me back to his cock, which he presses firmly into my mouth.

"Shhh. I'm in charge Nina."

He keeps his cock in my throat for a while. *Ok, ok! You're in charge! Release me!*

James keeps me there, fucks my throat, makes it clear who is in charge here, then he gets up and disappears. I take his place on the sofa, lay down and resume my selfish solo fun, on my back, my head backwards, my feet up. *Fuck you, James!*

"Where were we?"

James is back. Considering my position on the couch, I see him upside down. To tell the truth, I essentially see his cock stretched over me, and his balls from below. He caresses my chest, licks my breasts, then plays, making his cock brush my mouth. His hand supports my neck, and he gently pushes his limb down my throat. He comes and goes softly. I feel like a fuck doll as he basically fucks my mouth again, but the position is not unpleasant at all.

James groans. Without warning, he violently cums all over my body. A white line connects my neck to my pussy, the taste of his pleasure floods my tongue as a scream escapes from his throat.

James gives me his cock to clean up, keeps me on my back, head down, feet up. Then he sits close to me.

"So you swallow on the first night, right?"

Son of a bitch. I stay mute, then take his condoms with a sorry look, makes him understand that unfortunately for him he came too fast. *Go fuck yourself, James.* I get up, put a foot on the sofa and adjust my stockings one after the other. I catch my underwear on the floor, ready to leave. But a few seconds later James takes my hips.

His cock is hard again, glued to me. He grabs my hair with a soft but firm grip. His hand slams on my butt, I moan. He spanks me again, and again, then makes me bend and spreads my feet. He fingers me without warning. *Hmmmmm.*

Then he makes me sit on the table, puts a condom on his cock and slips it inside me. Not fully hard yet, but certainly big enough for me to moan.

"Gently, you're too big t ..."

Too late. James takes me violently. He pulls my hair back and goes so hard inside me that I feel like my pussy will be torn apart in less than a minute. He holds my throat, digs his tongue inside my mouth, and nails my pussy without restraints. My screams become uncontrollable, his cock is now back to hard, I feel full, owned, used, fucked like never.

Then my brain went blank. I yelled, and my voice broke. He grabbed the back of my neck and took my face in his shoulder as a long, violent and brutal orgasm made me lose my nerves. James kept pounding me, used and abused my pussy until my screams became a third orgasm with tears. He came inside me, but stayed in there, wrapped his hands around me, cuddled me and loved me with all the softness and care in the world. He held my body as long as it took for me to get myself back together, made sure I calmed down, made sure my tears disappeared, made sure I just didn't feel like the fucked bitch in his living room.

We stayed naked for a moment, even chatted on his couch like... friends, lovers, whatever. Then, without a word, I got dressed, kissed his cheek and stroked his hair before going home, my body totally excited and my legs shaking.

Of course, I wrote my phone number on the mirror with my lipstick and winked at him over my shoulder. I also left the black stockings he liked so much on his entrance door.

Five minutes later, my cell phone vibrated in my purse. From his window James waved with a smile, holding in his hand what looked like a black piece of cloth. *See ya, James!*

BONUS SHORT STORY:
WAY OUT OF YOUR LEAGUE

I was in a bar, alone. I was supposed to meet my friend Emy here for a drink, and then we were supposed to go to one of those black parties, where guests must come dressed in chic black outfits and only receive the meeting details at the last minute. Except Emy just sent me a text saying she had to cancel. And my phone ran out of batteries. So no address will come.

So I was at a very chic hotel's bar, wearing my favorite black dress, black tights, a stunning set of see-through black lingerie I put on for the occasion. *You never know, you might actually find a good excuse to get some fun back there...* But my evening was over.

"May I buy you a drink?"

I turned around, that cute guy was looking at me.

"What? Sorry? Who, me?"

He laughed, looked around, points at the empty bar with his finger.

"Yes, you..."

Of course, me, there's nobody at the bar. You stupid.

"Oh, well..."

I checked him out for a second. *Sure thing, handsome...*

"Thank you but no. I'm... expecting some friends."

He took the stool next to mine with a smile.

"Red wine?"

He didn't wait for my answer and nodded at the barmaid who came back a minute later with two glasses. *Hey, hold on! What on earth do you think you're doing here?* The lady poured wine inside the glass, gave me one with a polite smile. He looked at me. So did she.

I pushed my hair on my left shoulder, played with the glass, shook the wine gently inside it and then smelled it.

"Beautiful wine, thank you for the treat."

He smiled, looked at me, checked my cleavage and legs. *Wow wow wow, slow down.* I crossed my legs, looked at him in the eyes. *I'm not going to do the talking, handsome.*

"So, what brings you here? A ... beautiful girl sitting here alone... " - *Is he taking me for a call-girl? Seriously?*

I maintained eye contact, sipped my wine in silence.

"Nothing much, waiting for a friend who just cancelled."

I took my phone and shook it gently with a smile.

"I see"

But he wasn't buying my story.

"This is really too bad, you see, I... "

He sipped his wine, I brought my glass to my lips, bent my head, then looked at him straight in the eyes.

"You...?" - *He thinks I'm a call girl for real! He's blushing though, he's not used to it.*

"I actually thought you were... " - *Son of a bitch! Ok, let's play then.*

"Way out of your league? Yes... But thank you for the attention"

He opened his mouth, then closed it. *Touché*. I uncrossed my legs and pull on my dress. Then crossed my legs again, took the glass to my lips. *That's a funny game, but you'll need to do much better...* Then I looked at him again, bent my head on the side and brought my hair behind my ear.

"You were going to say something... "

I looked at him, waited for his answer. Brown hair, green eyes, handsome. Elegant, tailor-made suit, silk tie, nice watch. *Well well well, and I was going to give up on spending a nice evening... You might make my night Mr Handsome...*

The man checked my boobs and legs again, then he took a white envelope from his jacket, put it on the bar and pushed it to me.

"Can I convince you?"

I took the envelope and opened it. Dollars. Hundred dollars notes. Lots of them. *Son of a bitch! Well, I wasn't going to let you go but if you plan on playing that game...*

I pushed the envelope back on the bar, then looked at him.

"I believe I am definitely out of your league, Mr... But thank you again for that beautiful glass of wine. "

Then I stood, took my purse and walked away. *Come on, play with me, don't let me go...*

"Miss, please, wait" *Hmm, good boy.*

I stopped, turned around. He took my arm gently and slipped two envelopes in my purse. I smiled.

"Are you staying at this hotel then?"

Mr Handsome took my wrist gently, put my hand around his arm and took me into the elevator, then into his room. *Or should I say suite?* He closed the door behind us, turned around me, holding my waist. He lifted my hair, kissed the back of my neck. *Hmmm, now we're getting serious.*

I bent my head, gave him access while taking my shoes off. He unbuttoned my black dress, let it fall at my feet, then untied my bra and gently pushed me inside the suite, his hand in the bottom of my back. I hid my chest with my forearm, looked at him with a cheeky smile and moved into the room. He slipped a finger inside my thong.

"Wait, you won't need that thong in here."

I stopped, stayed put, my feet in line, and let him pull my thong down my legs. Then I stepped out, leaving the thong on the floor, and moved into the suite. Mr

Handsome looked at me, at every inch of my skin, brushed my shoulders, arms and butt with the back of his hands.

When he stopped, I turned around and faced him. I looked into his eyes, opened his shirt, opened his pants and got on my knees. I kissed his stomach, then covered his cock in little kisses until he began to react. I pulled his skin, took him inside my mouth and looked up into his eyes as my mouth swallowed him slowly but deeply.

He moaned, smiled. I released him, stroked his cock with my right hand.

"For the price, you can even hold my head, Mr Handsome" *Please, do it, play with me.*

He grabbed my boobs instead, played with my tits, patiently, until I moaned. I took him back, sucked him harder as his fingers drove me nuts. And then he took my head, took the lead, thrusting inside my mouth, rougher, deeper. Hmm, go on. I choked, he kept going. I could feel the head invading my throat as he pushed his based on my lips.

"Hmmmmpfff!"

I gagged, he released me, then lifted me up and took me to his bed. *Gentleman...* I sat there, opened my legs wide, and started to play with myself, looking into his eyes. He looked at me, considered my bald pussy and my black tights then opened a drawer and picked a condom.

"Now bitch, I'm going to fuck, the hell, out, of, you."
– Bitch? *Hmm, go on then, fuck, the hell, out, of...*

He placed the condom on his cock and grabbed my hips, patted my pussy with his cock, then slipped it inside me, holding me wide open. I groaned, flipped my head back, closed my hand around his cock as he penetrated me. He took me rough and wild, made sure my tights were open enough for him to see the penetration take place.

I grabbed the sheets, came violently but somehow managed to control my moans. He grabbed my hair. *Yes, pull my hair, go on, fuck me more.*

Then he flipped me over, pushed my stomach on the bed, took me deeper, held my body firmly and pulled my hair to make me arch my back. His cock brutalised my tight pussy, I began to yell.

I looked at the scene in the mirror in front of me, felt like I was somehow the hero of the hottest porn movie ever.

And then Mr Handsome moved faster. He pulled my

hair rougher and increased his thrusts violently. Until he made me cum. Again. *I can't stand it, it's too intense, finish me!*

"Aaaaaahhh! Fuck me! Please! Fuuuck meeee!!!"

My body exploded, my pussy erupted. I collapsed, he pounded my pussy a last time, then groaned and grabbed my waist. He came hard, smashed my butt twice, called me a bitch again. Then he pulled out of me, stood up, taking support on my lower back. My pussy felt empty at once, I moaned in pleasure once more.

Mr Handsome went for a shower, disappeared as the hot water began pouring, and left me there, fucked and soaked, without even a kiss.

I quickly put my bra on, and my dress, but I left my thong on the floor, right where he had left it. I also left the two envelopes there, with a little note on the floor. *Thank you for the orgasms, Mr handsome, but I really am out of your league...*

ABOUT THE AUTHOR

This book is the second volume of *My Lip-biting Short Stories Series*. The five short stories contained in this book have been written with a simple objective in mind, giving the readers an occasion to evade. I do hope that you have enjoyed them and that my ambition has been fulfilled.

If so, please leave me some stars and an encouraging comment on Amazon! It helps a lot! Thank you!

Yours,
Alex.

Made in the USA
Middletown, DE
13 June 2024